Call Me **Black**
Call Me **Beautiful**

Alicia Terry Henderson, Ph.D.

Illustrations by Jennifer C. Kindert

RoyalRegal

Royal Regal Books

To Kaitlyn
You are absolutely beautiful!
Alicia Terry Henderson
2003

To My Beautiful Angels - Raina and Ragan
You are my inspiration. Mommy loves you.

To My Biggest Fan - Leon
Thanks for believing in me and helping to make my dreams come true.
I truly appreciate all of your support. I love you.

To My Dear Parents - Theresa and Robert
Thank you so very much for providing me with a strong, loving environment;
one that has been most influential in the development of my positive sense
of individual and racial self. I love you guys.

- A.T. H.

To My Dad
Mom, Nicke and Grandma - thanks for being in my corner. Love, always.

- J.K.

To share your comments about
Call Me Black Call Me Beautiful
or to obtain copies, please write to:
Royal Regal Books
P.O. Box 973
Englewood Cliffs, New Jersey 07632
Or visit
www.royalregalbooks.com

ISBN 0-9719490-1-8
Library of Congress Control Number: 2002103531

First printing, August 2002

Printed in China by Palace Press International

This is Richard.

Richard loves school.
His favorite classes are
reading and music.
Richard also likes recess,
where he plays
soccer and basketball
with his friends Max and Bill.

Today, though, Richard
is feeling sad.
He can hardly wait until
the school day is done.
He just wants to go home
to see his mommy.

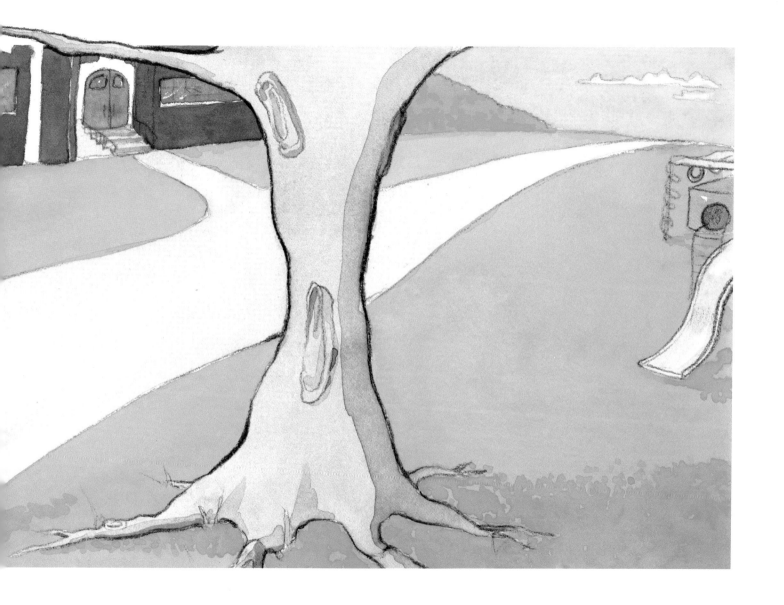

When the school bus arrives at
Richard's house,
he can see his mommy
looking for him
through the big
glass window
in the living room.

Richard springs from the bus,
pushes his way
through the front door,
and dashes into
his mommy's arms.

"**H**ello honey.
How was your day?"
asks Richard's mommy.

Richard puts his head down and walks
toward the kitchen.

His mommy follows him and begins to
prepare his snack.

It is clear that something is troubling Richard.

"Richard, are you OK? Why do you look so glum?" asks his mommy.

Richard looks into his mommy's eyes,
hesitating to speak.

"Go ahead sweetie,
tell me what's the matter."

Richard replies, "During recess today,
Max called me black."

"**W**hy did Max call you black?"
asks Richard's mommy.

"I don't know," says Richard.

"We were playing soccer
when all of a sudden
Max yelled out that I was black."

Richard's mommy pauses and responds,
"Well, honey, you are black."

Richard looks down at his hands and
arms and says matter-of-factly,

"No I'm not. I'm brown."

"**Y**es honey, you are brown,"
she agrees.
"You are my caramel brown baby.
Daddy is smooth, dark
chocolate brown, and
I am honey brown.

But people in our family
are called black,
though our skin color
is not actually the color black.

People in Max's family
are called white,
even though their skin
is not the color white."

"Why mama?" asks Richard.
"Why is our family called black
and Max's family called white?"

"**B**lack and white
are just colors used to describe
a family of people.

People with dark skin
are sometimes called black,
and people with light skin
are sometimes called white.

It's not a bad thing to be
called black or white,"
replies Richard's mommy.

She continues,
"Black people
are made with skin colors
of all shades of brown,
from the lightest brown
to the darkest brown.

This is what makes our
family so beautiful."

"**Y**ou mean dark brown
like grandpa Robert,
and light brown like
great-grandma Dorothy?"
says Richard with excitement.

"Yes, exactly,"
replies his mommy.

Now Richard feels proud to be called black.
Still, he wonders out loud,
"Are Max and his family beautiful too?"

His mother answers, "Yes dear.
Max and his family are also beautiful,
but in a different way.

So the next time that
Max calls you black,
smile at him with joy.

Explain to him that despite
your different skin colors,
you both have friendly hearts,
eyes, hands and feet,
and you are both
absolutely beautiful!"

Richard is not sad or confused anymore.
He is happy about being black.

In fact, he can't wait until tomorrow
so that he can go back to school
and tell Max that he is right -
that he is black, and
without a doubt, beautiful.

The End

About the Author

Alicia Terry Henderson is a child psychotherapist and lecturer of ethnocultural issues at the New York University Shirley M. Ehrenkranz School of Social Work. She has researched and written about the social psychological factors related to individual and black self-esteem development. *Call Me Black Call Me Beautiful* is her first children's book, and the first of her Multicultural Children's Book Series.

Alicia resides in Bergen County, New Jersey with her husband and two children.

●

About the Illustrator

Jennifer C. Kindert is a graduate of the Fashion Institute of Technology in New York City and the International Art School in Stockholm, Sweden. She is an illustrator and graphic designer.

Jennifer resides in New York City.